SO YOU WANNA KISS A GIRL...

CHRIS GAUCHER

 FriesenPress

Suite 300 - 990 Fort St
Victoria, BC, V8V 3K2
Canada

www.friesenpress.com

ISBN
978-1-4602-7801-7 (Hardcover)
978-1-4602-7802-4 (Paperback)
978-1-4602-7803-1 (eBook)

1. YOUNG ADULT FICTION, SOCIAL THEMES, DATING & SEX

Distributed to the trade by The Ingram Book Company

This is a work of fiction. Names, characters, places, and incidents are either the product of the author's imagination or are used fictitiously, and any resemblance to actual persons living or dead, business establishments, or locales is entirely coincidental.

TABLE OF CONTENTS

SO YOU WANNA KISS A GIRL...

Hi, I'm Liam. Liam Phillips. I'm 12 years old, and will soon be starting Grade 7. My mom is making me write this book as a summer project. She says it will be a useful experience. I think she just wants me off the computer. Really – she's making me write this the old fashioned way: paper, pen, and no spell check... I'm doomed! Anyway, I tried making a deal with her (I just love making deals!). I get one hour of screen time for every half an hour that I write. She says, "We'll see." I think the endless texts I get, mostly from girls, have freaked her out. We share a tablet – **MISTAKE**. Now, she can see my texts and emails. She says that she won't read them and that I have to trust her. She says that she has to trust me too. Who wants to read her boring texts from the phone company anyway?

We had "THE TALK" last year in school, which was followed by "THE TALK" at home. Too much information. All I want to do is go to a movie, and like, maybe kiss a girl. What's the big deal? Mom said that the first kiss is just the start and that I should know what I'm getting into. Her plan is to give me a lesson, every week for the entire summer, about "relationships" between boys and girls. I don't think I actually want one of those. They sound complicated. I'm supposed to write a chapter about each lesson. There are ten weeks of summer. How can telling me about girls take ten weeks? UGH!! Hey, half an hour is up... back to *Minecraft*, my favourite online game.

CHAPTER 1
Love Yourself...

I thought I'd better clarify the title of this chapter. It is **NOT** what you might be thinking. This book is rated G, so for any of **THAT** stuff please refer back to "**THE TALK**". Rather than "Love yourself," I actually prefer to say, "Like yourself." I think it is more appropriate. Anyway, Chapter One of "Mom's lessons about girls," here goes nothing.

Before you start liking a girl, it's best to feel okay about yourself. Otherwise, like I heard in a movie, "She'll rip you to shreds." That sounds nasty, in my opinion, no matter how cute she is. Mom says girls like boys who are cool in their own skin. This doesn't mean they act cool. This doesn't mean they think they are better than others. It just means that they are comfortable with who they are. They are confident, but not show offs. I was at the fair last week with a girl who's a friend, and a friend of hers came up and asked, "Why are you here with Liam?" She replied, "Why not?" Her friend said, "Because he's **SO** Liam."

I guess I could be offended by this, but when I stop and think about it, I *am* **SO** Liam. There's no one quite like me and I like it that way. I still make checklists in my head of all of my achievements, but Mom says one day I won't feel good about myself just because of my first place ribbons, trophies, medals, and "A"s.

I also won't feel bad about myself if I **DON'T** get those things. I will like me just because I am Liam. She says it is important to learn that, otherwise you will always be looking for compliments from a parent or eventually "the girl you wanna kiss." It's always nice to get compliments, but you are still the same person with or without them. You are also still the same person with or without the ribbons. I told Mom that this was getting a little deep for a 12-year-old, but I think I get what she was trying to tell me: If you can understand that you are good enough and lovable just for being *who you already are*, you won't be chasing multiple girls to make you feel good about yourself. It's kind of confusing, because at my age, I **WANNA** be chasing multiple girls. Even though I have a specific one picked out (next chapter), it is hard not to notice certain other ones. There are just so many cute ones and so many nice ones. Sigh, it's all so complicated. I'm surprised girls and boys get together at all!

I actually finished Chapter One! Yeah! It's my turn on the computer… just saying.

CHAPTER 2
Choosing the Girl

I've already done this. End of chapter.

But Mom…! Okay. I really, really like Megan. It's not like she has great hair or anything, but I like her because she likes me, or should I say **LIKED** me. She changes her mind every week. Mom says we'll talk about that in another chapter. Back to Chapter Two. Mom says that it is important to choose a girl who likes herself, who doesn't expect you to make her happy, and who doesn't need to be rescued (I think she's been watching too many Hollywood movies!).

Mom likes to quote popular songs from her youth when talking about the appearance of a girl. She wanted me to call this chapter "A 3 Dressed Up as a 9" (by a band called Trooper), or "She Ain't Pretty, She Just Looks That Way" (by the Northern Pikes). Cool band names, guys! I want to be in a band too one day!

So Mom has always told Katie and me (Katie is my 10-year-old sister) that it's what's on the inside that counts. This may apply to girls, but definitely not to Mexican pie – mushy beans, onions, peppers, and mystery meat – **YUCK**!! Anyway, back to girls. It is really hard, even at my age, to look at a pretty girl and not say "**WOW**!"

Hey! Did you ever notice that **WOW** is **MOM** spelled upside down? Maybe this is some kind of Freudian thing. My mom is always talking about Freud. For those of you who haven't heard of him, he was a type of doctor back in the very olden days – let's call him psychodude for short – who thought that all boys really loved their moms. Yeah, I know, **GROSS**. I mean I like my mom and love her too, in the way you say, "Love you, Mom," but not like **LOVE** love her! **WOW**, **MOM**, **WOW**, **MOM**, **WOW**, **MOM**. This is psycho… dude.

Okay, I'll start focusing.

Mom also told me not to judge a girl based on what she wears. She is actually pretty cool about girls wearing tight, short tops. A lot of my friends' parents think this is very inappropriate. I even heard one of them say a word that I don't think I'm allowed to write down. Mom just says, "You never know the circumstances, so you can't comment. Perhaps her little sister accidentally threw it in the dryer on high and it shrunk. Perhaps her family doesn't have a lot of money and it is last year's top and she grew." Sometimes I think my mom is a little naive, but she says that she's just trying to get a point across. She also says that just because a girl's top is tight, it doesn't mean she deserves any less respect than a girl dressed in a baggy sweatshirt. Girls need to "find themselves," she says, and explore all parts of who they are. Then she looks at me and winks, "But this doesn't mean that **YOU** have to explore all their parts – even if they **ARE** out there for all to see." (Now, is this non-judgemental?)

She says a girl, like a boy, has to feel comfortable in her own skin. I'm still not exactly sure what this means, but she says it all comes back to liking who you are. I think Megan more than likes herself, because she's always acting like she's the best at everything. I do admit that I find this somewhat annoying, but still, there's something about her… I think it's because she likes me. She gets who I am. She's not constantly trying to change me. Some girls want you to dress a certain way, act a certain way, and be a certain way. With Megan, I can just be me – that's cool.

The last biggest thing about choosing the girl is that she needs to treat you with respect. There's no point in pursuing someone who always calls you a doofus, for example. This is a word that has been flying around school a lot lately. I'm not allowed to write down any other bad names, but I'm sure you know a few more. Mom says that name-calling is an automatic warning sign of someone not being nice on the inside. She has zero tolerance for it and says it has no place in a relation-ship. She also says she **NEVER** wants to hear me call a girl a bad name. She must be speaking from experience, because her eyes get really big and she speaks her words very clearly. She says we need to have a separate chapter just on criticism and contempt, called the "A, B, "C"s of Relationships." **UGH**! I'm barely through Chapter Two! Please mom, stop talking. Why do moms and girls go on and on and on and on and on…? My brain only has so much space.

Good news: My half hour is up! See you next week. ☺

CHAPTER 3
To Smell Me is to Love Me

So, you're a healthy, confident boy. You've chosen the girl. Ready, set, **GO** – Oops, that's the last chapter – seven chapters away. What else do I possibly need to know? Well, Mom wants me to devote an entire chapter to hygiene! She insists that the likelihood that a girl will actually kiss me will increase exponentially (that means a lot) if I smell good, or at least don't smell at all. I remember going to last year's school Christmas concert, after I had used my step-dad John's coconut shampoo. All of the girls wanted to sit next to me and kept smelling and touching my hair. I actually think that was the start of all of this boy/girl stuff. They noticed me. I liked the attention. Need I go on?

So why have I not continued on this smelling-good track? It's high maintenance, man! I play soccer; I smell. I skateboard; I smell. A boy could wash himself 24/7 and still smell. Mom says that if I don't get it down now, when my hormones kick in it will be even worse. She forces me to shower at least twice a week when I'm at her house. I now own deodorant, wash my feet with soap, and occasionally use this vanilla body spray my sister says smells good. Deciding on a scent is really hard, because there are so many products to choose from: men's, unisex, cologne, aftershave, eau de toilette... I'm glad Mom is footing the bill, because it would use all of my allowance and then some.

It took me a while, but I finally found the perfect scent. I don't know if I'm allowed to write brand names in my book, but let's just say that it's well known. Now I get grief from my mom and my sister that I am using too much of it and putting it places where I shouldn't. I keep a bottle in the car just to drive them crazy. Katie freaks; my mom opens all of the windows, and I get a lecture on how to apply scents properly: They do not go on the outside of your clothes; you do not use half a bottle at once; and if you can smell it on yourself, you are using too much. **NICE**. I do as I'm asked and try to smell good and I still get dumped on... **UGH**!

I forgot to mention that, when my mom is not busy telling me what to do, she is fixing teeth (she's a dentist). So, of course, she insists that fresh breath is required for that all-important first kiss. She tells me what she tells all of her teenage patients: "Floss your teeth and smell the floss." **YUCK**! Then she adds, "This is what others are smelling when you kiss them, if you don't floss your teeth." She says it works every time. They all start flossing!

I think the whole smelling-good issue is overrated. Personally, I think someone just wanted to get rich. Look back in history. Do you think the Romans actually cared about how they smelled? They only bathed once a year! Come to think of it, a lot of them got eaten by lions – Hmmm... Mom, I'm next in the shower!

CHAPTER 4
Trust Me... Honest

I think Mom is making me write this chapter because lately I've been, what she calls, "stretching the truth." She asks me why I lie, and I kind of freeze. It's not like I do it on purpose. It just happens. The other day, she told me to have a shower while she took Katie to art class. I had to do this before I could have screen time. She said that I could have a quick one. She didn't specify that I actually needed to use shampoo. When she came home, she smelled my hair and said, "I don't smell any shampoo. Did you wash your hair?" I sheepishly said, "Yes." I had wet my hair and patted my head a few times with my soapy hands... so I sort of washed my hair. If she knew I didn't do it, why did she ask me in the first place? Mom has super radar for lying. I told an even bigger stretch of the truth last week, so I'm walking on thin ice.

Mom says that honesty is very important to learn. It can make or break a relationship. There's that "R" word again. If I want to kiss a girl, I need to be able to be honest. Does this mean I tell her if I don't like her haircut? I really don't think that will get me to first base. I decided to seek a man's advice on this topic and went to my step-dad. John is really cool. He is very nice to

Katie and me, and he makes my mom happy. (Okay Mom, I'll rephrase that, since a boy isn't supposed to *make* a girl happy.) My mom seems happier since John has been a part of our lives. Is that okay?

John never says a mean thing. He always thanks Mom for dinner and tells her it's great. Sometimes I wonder if taste buds really do change with age or if he's eating the same stuff as me.

I asked him, when my mom wasn't around, if he's being honest. He said that what he's being is "not critical." He tried to compare it to me getting a "C" on my report card. (Just for the record, French aside, I'm an "A" student – for any of you girl readers out there who think that's cool and haven't got the "non-judgmental" concept yet.) Back to the story... so if I got a "C", John said I wouldn't feel very good if my mom or he told me how terrible this was. He said that I would know myself if this wasn't my best, and if it wasn't, I would probably feel lousy. What good would it do for my mom or him to go on about it? He said that the same is true about my mom's cooking. She knows when the broccoli is mushy, so what good does it do to focus on what isn't good about the meal? Instead he thanks her for making the meal, says that something else tastes good, and dinner goes smoothly. Well, except for the occasional drama from Katie!

But what about a haircut? Do I tell a girl what I think? John said that, when my mom gets a haircut, he tells her that she looks nice and asks her how **SHE** likes it. Hair will always grow and there will be lots of time in the future to tell her he likes it better at a different length. But he emphasized that it doesn't really matter if he likes it or not. What matters is that **SHE** likes it. If she doesn't like it, he can try to make her feel better by saying that it will grow, but to go on about how ugly it actually is doesn't make anyone happy. He said that, as you grow up, you have to know that what others think of you really doesn't matter in comparison to what you think of yourself. And he added that, if they treat you differently because of a haircut, or a "C", or mushy broccoli, they don't deserve to be kissed by you in the first place. Then he winked.

So I'm still a little confused about the whole honesty thing, but I think it can be summed up like this: If you get that "don't want to get busted", "got to protect yourself" feeling in the pit of your stomach, then **DON'T LIE**. It will always come back to bite you. But if being totally honest could cause hurt feelings, find a creative, nicer way to let the person know what you think. Sometimes the truth isn't easy to hear, but it is important for a person to know. It may not be essential to tell someone you don't like their haircut, but if you don't like how someone is treating you or others, that person needs to be told. It's also important to be able to tell a girl how you honestly feel about her. Hmmm, feelings... this is getting complicated again. I think I hear the computer calling me.

CHAPTER 5
Hormones 101

And now the chapter you've all been waiting for – or maybe not. Mom insists that this is **THE** most important chapter for understanding women (girls, at my age). Mom thinks hormones are responsible for 90% of her moods. I'm not sure if this is a hyperbole (a fancy word for a big exaggeration – just tucking in a little grammar for bonus Mom points), but I get the message that this is big stuff. She believes a lot of females don't realize how much hormones affect them, but if men (boys) and women (girls) had a better understanding of hormones, the world of relationships would be a happier place. This doesn't mean that hormones are the only reason a girl's mood may change. School, friends, parents, and homework are just a few examples of what can cause ups and downs for both girls and boys. I'm sure you could add to this list. Hormones, however, can make problems seem even worse. Boys have hormonal changes too. You may have noticed your voice getting deeper, muscles growing, hair appearing where it wasn't before, and lots of thoughts about girls. Did I mention lots of thoughts about girls?

Anyway, back to girls and their hormones. Not all females are affected equally (probably a good thing). Mom says that I have to review the biology info from "**THE TALK**." Here's the skinny: From about age 12 until about age 50, a girl releases an egg every month (ovulation is the scientific word for this). For about two weeks before this and several days after, she's usually happy and seems to like you a lot. When the egg doesn't get fertilized, her hormones shift, and her moods can start to change. This is what happens for almost two weeks, until a girl gets her period, and then the whole cycle starts again.

Mom re-emphasized that every girl is different in terms of how much her moods change and for how long. This is just meant to be a guide. **PMS**, or premenstrual syndrome, is the name given to the symptoms a girl may have before she gets her period. Mood changes, such as anger, irritability, and sadness aren't the only possible symptoms, but they are the ones that can affect us boys the most. Mom says that it's important for boys to understand what girls sometimes go through during this time.

Now this is a very delicate and controversial subject. It is my understanding that you are **NEVER** supposed to mention **PMS** to a girl/woman. Mom made sure I knew this. I told her that one day a teacher had a yelling fit at my friend Sean. Mom explained that perhaps she was having a bad day or that maybe she was having a hormonal moment. "But," she added, "don't raise your hand

and ask her if she's getting her period." Mooooomm!!
She pointed out that it is important for a boy to be aware
of what a girl may be going through, but it's very disrespectful to assume that a girl's moods are only because
of her hormones.

Mom said that it's a good idea to know about a girl's
cycle if you are dating. She said that one time she found
John's daybook, and noticed her name written down,
with the words "day 17" beside it. She didn't know what
this meant at the time, but John told her (in a nice way)

that this is a day in the month when he thinks she's particularly hormonal. He had been charting her for a while and found out that there seemed to be a pattern. (Note: this day is not the same for all girls; it's just what John found out about my mom.) He always buys her flowers on "day 17," and on that day he's never offended by what she says, even though it's usually nasty. He says to himself, "She'll like me tomorrow or the next day." I should let Jay Z and Justin Timberlake in on this information, because I don't think they know. In their song "Holy Grail," they sound pretty confused about a girl loving them one day and not the next.

Now a girl may not tell you if she's getting or has her period, because it's private and she may even be embarrassed by it, but you can do some charting like John did and figure it out. (I'm a math guy so I love charting.) It's pretty easy. Some warning signs might be: She suddenly seems to not like you and criticizes a lot of things you do; she gets upset easily; she doesn't want you to touch her – even holding her hand may give her the creepy crawlies. Mom tells me that there's usually a day or two in her cycle when she feels like bugs are crawling all over her skin. I think I should sell "**DON'T TOUCH ME**" T-shirts. It would be much clearer to everyone and I could make a lot of money, considering how many girls there are in the world.

Mom believes that once you see a girl's pattern, you are well on your way to relationship bliss. You'll even know the perfect time to try to kiss a girl so that she

will actually want to kiss you back. You'll know, when she snaps at you for not getting butter on her popcorn, to say, "Oh, I'm sorry, I'll go back and get you some," rather than snapping back and saying, "I just spent an hour in line for you and this is the thanks I get? Go get it yourself!"

You see, in the first two weeks of her cycle, it doesn't seem to matter if you forget the butter; she'll probably not comment or will eat it anyway, but on a different day, or a different week, it's a different story. It's up to us boys to adapt, especially if we want to kiss a girl. In some ways, I think it's better to be a guy, because even though you have to be extra kind sometimes, you don't feel like you have bugs on you, or that your head is going to explode, or that you are going to turn mean. You also don't get cramps unless you eat too much pizza and pop.

You can practise figuring all this charting stuff out with your mom. Then you'll know when to ask her for that phone you've been wanting. Now she may not remember agreeing to it when she hits "day 17," but it's worth a try. Maybe I can invent an app to keep track of the cycles of every girl I know. It could give me warning signs, so I'd know when it would be a better idea just to hang with the boys. I could make millions if this took off...

Back to reality. As I said earlier, Mom has quite the hormonal thing going on. She says it's because she's entering **MENOPAUSE** – the time when women stop having periods forever. I think it's called this, because they should take a pause from men – seriously!! No men. I don't much like being around my mom when she's crying or yelling, which lately is more of the time than I would like. What's really weird is that it all happens in a split second. One minute she's laughing and then **BOOM** – all this over-the-top stuff comes out of her mouth. Don't get me wrong, I love my mom, but it is a little strange. She tells me I have to be able to know when her upset is really about me and when it's just the hormones. She tries to tell me when it's not about me, so I don't feel bad about myself and stuff. Mom calls feeling bad about yourself "going to the badlands." She says I have to be careful not to "go to the badlands," because I could get stuck there for the rest of my life. Lost me again, Mom. I thought the Badlands was a place in South Dakota. I don't think I want to go there forever.

Anyway, girls/women usually get their periods for about thirty-eight years, times twelve months, so I guess that's how long I will have to deal with this stuff.

It's like a roller coaster. I think even the Mindbender at West Edmonton Mall is less scary than this! Speaking of roller coasters, I think I'm going to go build one on *Minecraft*. I definitely need a break after this chapter.

INTERMISSION

WOW, you won't believe what happened... twelve months happened! What I mean is, remember when I said it couldn't possibly take ten weeks to learn about girls? Well it takes even longer! The good news is that I've had more time to write this. I wrote the first five chapters and then Mom decided that I needed a "field trip." That is, I needed to take a break and get some real-life experiences. Her lecturing, I mean teaching me, the ins and outs of girls is just theory. She thought it would be interesting to add some personal stories. I am now 13 and in Grade 8. Even in a year, my thoughts on girls have changed plus I have increased hands-on knowl-edge. Unfortunately, Mom's making me talk about the upsets. **WOW**... can't we just move on?

I've changed in other ways too. These days I am known by my *Minecraft* nickname **LP**slaayer. I am the lead singer of my band, which is called "**DIGGING FOR DIAMONDS**" (with my two best friends, Sean on drums and Jayden on bass). My hair is unfortunately a little on the short side. The hair stylist didn't quite understand the word "trim" and my specific instructions not to show any ear. Mom says that it will grow. In the meantime, I'll wear my favourite toque, even though it's not winter. *Minecraft* now shares time with Facebook, YouTube, and "I just want to be alone" time.

A lot has happened in a year, but to catch you back up, I'll summarize 13-year-old me in regards to the first five chapters:

1 I'm learning that I'm a pretty cool guy just the way I am (what's not to like? haha).

2 Megan, well, let's just say those were the good old days – now she won't even talk to me. ☹

3 Hormones have kicked in. I hate to admit it, but Mom was right about the smell stuff, and (just for the record) I do not use my sister's vanilla spray anymore.

4 I've been working on the honesty stuff, but I wish I had reread that chapter before the whole break up happened (details to follow in Chapter Six).

5 Mom's menopause is in full swing, and I can't keep up with the moods of the girls at school so I don't even try. Thank goodness Katie is only 11. I've never ever wanted off a roller coaster ride as badly as I want off this hormonal one. Did you ever notice that **HOR**rifying, **HOR**rid, **HOR**rendous, all start with the same three letters as **HOR**monal? This is **NOT** a coincidence!!!

When I'm done the app, to help you make sense of it all, you'll be the first to know. Anyway, back to the story, I still want my screen time before I'm forced to go to bed. Enjoy!!

CHAPTER 6
Apology NOT Accepted

Girls have memories even better than elephants. I just don't get it. You do something wrong, and you apologize; they say they accept your apology, but **NOOO**.... The next time you do something wrong, you have to not only apologize for the "new" wrong but also for the "old" wrong, not to mention for every other wrong you ever did. I'm still apologizing for pulling someone's hair in Grade 1! Who can remember Grade 1? It seems to me that girls can always remember the bad things you did, but can they remember all of the times you were nice to them, bought them treats, or took them to a movie? Why do they even bother telling you they accept your apology, when it seems to me that it's apology **NOT** accepted?

There also seems to be a particular formula for apologizing to girls. If you don't word it just the way they want to hear it, it's not good enough. They then end up giving you the silent treatment, telling not only their friends what a jerk you are, but also anyone else they can think of on Facebook. That's what happened to me. Remember back a year ago when I talked about Megan? Well, truth is we dated for a few months, broke up, got back together, and then I realized that I only got back with her to please her friends. I really wasn't that into her anymore – not that there was anything wrong with her, but even if there was, I wouldn't have posted it on Facebook. Just because I liked someone else does not make me a horrible person. There's no sense pretending to like someone and having it go on for months. It doesn't make it any easier for anyone. So now she hates me, her friends hate me, and she's trying to make every girl alive hate me. I think she figures that if she can't have me, then she doesn't want anyone else to either... but that could just be my big ego talking (you know, that voice in your head that tells you how great you are). So what do you do? This is just one girl. I apologized for hurting her feelings, but what else can I do? UGH!! Why do girls stick together so much?

I was the one who decided that there had to be a chapter about this. See how much I've grown in a year? I need to know apology basics and I think every boy needs to know them too. I decided I should talk to John again. I thought about asking my mom, but she's a girl and I'd probably end up apologizing for wanting to know. I don't even know if my mom knows how apologizing works, because if she did, wouldn't she just start accepting my apologies and stop going on and on and on?

For example, the other day I called Katie a nipple. It's what my friends and I have recently started calling each other. I don't really know why. We often say, "Hey, you nipple!" We also use it for describing other people who are, well… you know… idiots. Anyway, I called my sister this and I got a big lecture from my mom on how disrespectful I was being. The next day, I played soccer and there were some less than sportsmanlike players on the other team. After the game, we went to the concession stand and I whispered to Katie, "There's that nipple from the other team." Well Mom's hearing may be going, but she had no problem hearing that. She said, "**WHAT** did you say?" She knew what I said. Why do parents always do this? She went on to say that she does not reward this type of behaviour. Then she stood in line, not saying another word (aka the silent treatment), and bought Katie her treat. I didn't get anything, of course. When we got back to the car, she gave me an earful. She basically told me the same stuff she had said the night before, but in a much louder voice. What can a guy do?

She said that I was trying to push her buttons. Sometimes I think moms/girls give us too much credit, convinced that we're these grand planners whose mission is to try to get them to explode. Who wants to be at the receiving end of an explosive mom or girl? Not me.

So I apologized by saying sorry to Katie and my mom, but it didn't do any good. Every time I asked for

something, like if we could stop for pizza on the way home, Mom kept bringing up that she was not going to reward me and that there were consequences for my actions. So when does it end? When they've decided that you've had enough punishment or when they finally believe that you are sorry? **UGH**!!!

As I said, I went to John.

I rarely hear John and my mom arguing, so maybe he's figured out how to get my mom to stop going on about things if he's done something wrong. He agreed with me that most girls do hold onto things longer than boys do. He said that could just be a difference between males and females, but he believes that there are some things a guy can do when apologizing to make things better. He also believes that, at certain times of the month, there's nothing a guy can really do except to try not to mess up in the first place. (That's where the charting comes in handy.) John talked a bit too long, so I decided to just list the main steps of an epic apology.

1) Sooner is better than later, but not too soon. By this I mean that you don't automatically say you are sorry as soon as you realize you've done something wrong, because a simple "I'm sorry" lacks meaning.

2) Look her in the eye – even hold her hands (unless it's your mom).

3) Express your apology sincerely (not like Eminem does in his song "Love the Way You Lie,") – Girls will know when you're just apologizing to get them to like you again or to get them to stop talking.

4) Admit you were wrong (if you were). Sometimes this is a little hard to do – actually, more than a little. This is also the step where you might feel a bit ashamed, because there's a part of you that wished you had acted differently. Don't

worry; we all mess up. You have your whole life to keep learning.

5) Say that you will try your very best not to do it again, if it's something you could repeat.

6) Show understanding for her feelings, but know that they are "her feelings." This is where John lost me a little. He tried to explain that a girl can *choose* how she reacts to what you've done, and said that you can also *choose* how you react if she gets upset. I think he's trying to say that you shouldn't judge her feelings or tell her she's over-reacting, because she gets to feel whatever she wants to feel. But at the same time, you don't have to keep beating yourself up because of how she reacts. She might need time to figure out what she feels. Sometimes talking with her helps it hurt less. Listen to what she needs to tell you.

So this is what it sounds like when you put it all together:

"I'm really, really sorry for doing such and such. (This is where you put in what you did wrong.) I was wrong to do what I did. I care about your feelings and will do my best to not do it again. I understand how you could be hurt by it. I didn't mean for it to hurt you. Do you need to talk?"

Remember, it's best to apologize in person. If you have no choice but to text or talk on the phone, keep to the formula as much as possible and make a point of telling her you can talk about things more when you see her next.

You don't need to go on about the million reasons (excuses) why you did what you did. Just admit you were wrong to do it. Don't try to blame anyone. John says to make it for her, not for you. This may help her forgive you and not bring it up the next time you mess up. I wish I had followed John's advice when I broke up with Megan. I would have left out the steps where I say I was wrong and that I wouldn't do it again, but letting her know that I didn't want to hurt her, and saying I understood why she was hurt, may have made it easier for her. It may also have stopped her from spreading stories about me on Facebook. I think I could write an entire chapter on breaking up, but that will be in my next book, *You've Kissed a Girl, So Now What*? I've got to finish writing this one first.

CHAPTER 7
WOW, She Likes My Friend

So this chapter is also mostly my idea. Mom asked me what my biggest questions are about girls. One is, why do girls always change their minds, and another is why do they always like my friends better? Once again, I zoned out for part of her lesson. Some of her answers were longer than I needed, and some I just plain don't get, but they will fill the pages and I'll be one chapter closer to finishing this book!

Part of why girls change their minds may have to do with their hormones, but assuming hormones are under control (this can now be classified as a fantasy novel – just kidding, Mom), there are a few other reasons a girl may like you one day and not the next. Mom uses the phrase, "Boys pursue and girls choose." This is why you often see boys chasing girls around the playground in elementary school. In Grade 8, you don't usually see the physical chase, but you do see the boys trying to get the girls' attention in various ways – often embarrassing themselves in the process. (Sound familiar, Sean and Jayden?)

It's very competitive at school, because all of these 13-year-olds are together in a fairly small space. Apparently, even at this age (whether they know it or not) boys and girls are worried about finding a mate, and so the competition begins. It's built in. It's biology. It's what contributes to the survival of the human race (okay, I'm getting a bit carried away). Girls want to find the best mate possible, so they like someone until someone with better genes (not jeans!) comes along – or at least someone who they **THINK** has better genes.

Genes are like a set of instructions that help determine how we look, and lots of other stuff about us. Certain characteristics are passed from our parents to us through genes. (Not sure if you've taken this in science yet. I had to look it up.) Anyway, so how do you compete with the guy with a six-pack or a friend who always makes girls laugh more than you do? Do you start doing sit-ups? Do you become a comedian?

Firstly, you have to stop comparing yourself constantly with your friends. Part of this goes back to Chapter 1 – "Love Yourself..." You also can't let it bother you if a particular girl you like is more into your friend. Not every girl is going to like you and that is okay. Decrease the jealousy – green doesn't look good on anyone. Instead, be the kind of person a girl would want to choose. There are certain traits that will make you more appealing.

In general, girls like to be listened to. Sometimes this is hard, when all you want to ask is, "Are you done yet?" – especially when they repeat themselves a lot. It's interesting, because they never seem to forget anything **WRONG** that you did, but they can't remember that they just told you the same thing three times. Anyway, the point is to be genuinely interested in them and let them talk. Don't always talk about **YOUR**self and **YOUR** achievements. Girls often want to know that you like them and that they are special. This is tricky, because if they think you are too into them, they may back off and choose someone who's harder to get, but if you don't tell them enough times how much you like them, they might complain to their friends and ditch you anyway. Hmmm... seems like there's a very fine line here.

Mom says that another important thing to really understand is that, for a girl, the first kiss may be more emotional than physical. That's why everything leading up to that moment – the listening, the being interested, the making her feel special (the emotional) – sets the stage so that, even if the kiss itself (the physical) is less than perfect, she can walk away feeling incredible. Boys, on the other hand, often depend more on the physical to feel incredible. But trust me, once you see that smile on her face, that sign that she's into you, it's all good. You also may not get a charge from every girl you kiss. Sometimes it takes a while to find that certain someone you connect with, and sometimes it takes a while for that charge to happen – and that's okay. You might just need more time to make the kiss a special one, and not just a "quick kiss behind the school dumpster" one.

As far as friendship goes, it's not worth losing a friend just to kiss a girl. However, true friends don't make you choose between them and a girl, and a girl worth kissing doesn't make you choose between her and your friends. You both need friends. You also have to let friends choose whom they wanna kiss. You may have your own opinion, just like they do. Remember not to make too many comments – sometimes they have to figure things out on their own. **AND**, if you really think they are making a mistake, buy them a copy of this book and highlight Chapter 2 – "Choosing the Girl," in bright yellow!! Come to think of it, I had better keep extra copies for Sean and Jayden ☺ – just saying.

Since these chapters are getting longer, and require more research, I think it's time to renegotiate the deal with my mom. Mom? Oh Mom…?

CHAPTER 8
The A, B, "C"s of Relationships

Glad I renegotiated before writing this one… I'm up to two hours of screen time for every chapter now. ☺

Apparently there are a lot of "C" words that apply to relationships. I'm very glad that when Mom suggested this chapter, it was only the letter "C" I had to focus on. For a minute there I thought I'd have to go through the whole alphabet. There are good "C"s and not so good "C"s. Something like good news and bad news. Let's start with the not so good "C"s. Mom says that these are things like criticism, contempt, conflict, and competition. She says that they are some of the biggest reasons boy/girl relationships don't work out. They are also warning signs of someone whom you **DON'T** wanna kiss.

Criticism can be positive – such as when your teacher tells you how you could make your project better. However, the type of criticism that can be hurtful is when you judge someone in a mean way. Mom says that sometimes people criticize others because it makes them feel better about themselves; sometimes they criticize to make you feel bad about yourself, and some-times it's just what they've grown up with and they can't or don't see it as being wrong. But it is wrong. It's okay to offer an opinion on something when asked, but to constantly be negative about what someone does, says, looks like, or even how they kiss, is just not cool. When you are constantly criticized, you don't feel like you can do anything right and you start not liking yourself very much. Before this happens, you have to remember everything you learned in the first chapter. Sometimes you might think a girl is so "hot" that you don't care if she criticizes you, but trust me, no girl is worth feeling like a loser.

Remember, "not criticizing" applies to you too. In our Internet world of thumbs up, thumbs down, and endless comments, it's easy to think it's normal and okay to comment and criticize, but actually nothing good comes from it. I'm thinking of starting my own social media site called "No Comment," because I don't need to know what everybody thinks of me, good or bad. It doesn't change who I am. I think some social media sites should be named "Dumpster", because they end up being a place where people put their crap. Actually maybe "Outhouse" would be more accurate.

Anyway, back to the "C"s. (Actually crap does start with "C" Mom!)

Contempt. This is another word for hatred. If someone tells you they hate you, it's like the haunted house whose walls bleed the words "GET OUT!" Seriously, run fast in the other direction. According to Mom, yelling and hatred can be a cover up for the hurt a person feels inside, but she says that people have to figure out their own hurt. You can't fix it for them. When they are okay with themselves, they may be okay to kiss. In the meantime, stick to the ones who don't take their anger out on you.

I have an "**I LOVE HATERS**" T-shirt, but that doesn't mean I want to kiss them!! If you are the one who feels hate inside, it's best to talk with someone who can help you, before you find a girl you wanna kiss. I do feel for you really, but girls aren't there to take your stuff out on... or to make it all better for you.

Conflict is the next word on the list. Conflict (or as you may call it, "a battle") is tricky. Mom says that there is bound to be some conflict in a relationship, partly because you are a boy and she is a girl, and partly because you are two different people often brought up with different values and ideas. There is healthy (good) conflict and unhealthy (bad) conflict. Healthy conflict is when you disagree about things, but at the end of talking together, you both learn a little. This doesn't mean you change each other's mind or try to say that your opinion is better; it just means that you realize there may be more than one way of looking at things. Mom wanted to prove her point about this idea, so she showed me a picture and asked, "What do you see?" I said, "I see an old woman." She said, "I see a young woman." I looked again and still saw an old woman. Then mom outlined an image of a young woman that was hidden within the picture. It was freaky. The picture had both a young woman and an old woman in it. Neither of us was right or wrong, we just saw it differently. Sometimes there's more than one way to look at a situation, and if during conflict, you can see this, it's healthy.

Unhealthy conflict is when you argue, think the other person is wrong and stupid, and don't respect that there's more than one way of looking at things. You might stomp away or give the silent treatment, and you may even kick, throw, or break something – not healthy. Before it gets to that point, you should say, "Let's agree to disagree," and maybe take a deep breath. Mom says that sometimes stepping away from an argument gives you a chance to look at the whole picture, so that the next time you talk about it, things are a little calmer. Unhealthy conflict doesn't mean that you have to break up. It just means you have to change the behaviour to make it healthier.

Competition can also be good or bad. Sometimes competition makes us try a little bit harder at something, but if you are competing just to show that you are better than another person (in this case a girl), then you need to go back to Chapter One. If you say you are smarter, faster, funnier, a better this, a better that, and do things to prove that fact, then give your head a shake. Likewise, if a girl is always trying to be better than you and lets you know it, then also give your head a shake. Learn to celebrate (another "C" word!), what she can do and what you can do, and know that no one has to be better. My mom told me a story about her and her ex-boyfriend playing tennis together on some tropical island. I guess it was like forty degrees Celsius and the court was made of asphalt (that adds up to it being like an oven). To make a long story short, they were so competitive that they refused to end on a tie and the games kept going until my mom ended up with second-degree burns on her legs (that's really bad ☹). I'm not sure if they finally just quit, or if someone won, but this is definitely an example of unhealthy competition.

Now onto the good "C"s. I've already mentioned celebrating. The other good "C"s are contribution, conversation, and communication. (Sorry if this sounds Confusing!) Celebrating means being happy for the other person's achievements. You can celebrate someone just by saying, "Good job." Even though I've told you that we have to be able to like ourselves without needing pats on the back from other people, complimenting others when they do well is just a nice thing to do. It's also important to realize that it's okay for a girl to shine more than you. Sometimes you shine; sometimes she shines, and you can both celebrate each other. Often times there is a "one-up-man-ship" (as Mom calls it) in relationships. This goes back to competition. A girl does something well, and then you say something that makes you look a bit better. For example, if she runs a 10K race in an hour and feels good about it, and then you say, "Good for you, but I ran it in 47 minutes," it kind of takes away from the celebration. Remember, it's not about you – hard concept, I know...

Contribution is a bit harder to understand. Mom claims if you are going to have a girlfriend, you have to make the relationship important and contribute. It's not like school; you don't get bonus marks just for showing up. Contribution doesn't mean you have to give a girl gifts. You can contribute by helping, sharing, or doing something nice to make her life easier. It's reciprocal, which means she should contribute too. You don't have to contribute exactly the same amount or exactly the same things (even-steven), but you both need to feel okay with what the other is contributing. I know that, even in our home, Mom tells us that we all have to contribute at dinner time, whether it's setting the table, cooking the meal, or loading the dishwasher. It can't always be left up to one person. She says the same is true for a relationship. The amount you each contribute may change day to day and that's okay. However, if you find that you are not contributing at all, you have to ask yourself if you are really into this girl or not, or if you are really ready for this. Relationships take work and compromise (another "C" word, oh no!!!). If you feel that she is not contributing, you also have to ask if she is the one for you.

Conversation and communication pretty much go together. It's important to be able to talk with each other. As I said earlier, girls like to talk and sometimes they need you just to listen. Other times they want you to help them solve their problems or just want to tell you about their day. They may also want you to talk about feelings, which for a lot of boys is, well... you know, awkward. I often hear Mom ask John, "What do you think about that?" or "How does that make you feel?" John told me he wished he knew the "language of girls" way back when, because he thinks it is different from that of boys. Sometimes sharing for boys means sharing sports scores or what they ate for lunch. Not that there's anything wrong with this, but this is definitely different from what a girl may want to talk about.

You can have a good conversation, as long as you can both respect each other and don't ask, "Why do you **ALWAYS** talk about such and such...?" Or "Why do you **NEVER** want to talk about your feelings...?" Accept the

fact that girls are very different from boys in many ways, but this doesn't mean better or worse.

Mom says good communication means you listen and try to understand what's important to each other without judging; you don't hurt the other person on purpose with your words or actions, and you let the other person know what interests you. It means you can be real. Sometimes it's hard for a boy to really know what he's feeling because, to be honest, we don't spend a lot of time thinking about what we are feeling. It probably goes back to the days when we were hunters and we didn't or couldn't spend too much time thinking about feelings or our prey would kill us. Kind of funny when you think of it, because nowadays if we don't spend enough time thinking about our feelings, we will be ditched by our prey (the girl we are pursuing), which I'm sure hurts just as much. When is evolution going to catch up?

Communication is also non-verbal. It can be the way you smile at each other or a look that means back off. It can be the way you hold each other's hand. Mom says it is important to have good communication when you wanna kiss a girl, because it's helpful to know how she likes to kiss. Believe it or not, there are different styles of kissing and what you like may not be what she likes. If you can talk about it, as awkward as it is, you can figure out together what makes it good for both of you. Now I don't want you to get all freaked out about technique and be more nervous than you are already, but try not to get offended if she tells you what she likes. It doesn't mean you are doing something wrong. It's just a way for her to let you know what feels good for her. Mom says this will all make more sense once I write the second book. There she goes again. Can I please just get through writing the first one?

Good timing for me, I'm finally done with this chapter. Onto the Computer Mom – another "C" word!

CHAPTER 9
A Certain Soda Pop and Other Myths...

After such a long, deep chapter, you get to be rewarded with a little humour. The basis for this chapter all began when I heard at school that a certain soda pop, which shall remain nameless, causes your penis to shrink. It was a reliable source (my best friend Sean) who told me this, so of course, I believed it to be true. I decided to bring it up at the dinner table. My mom burst out laughing and told me it was definitely not true; in other words, it's a myth. She then went into this long talk about how she read on the Internet that caffeine (an ingredient in this soft drink) might affect a boy's sperm, but that it does not actually make the penis smaller. I wondered how I could justify putting this information into my book, just in case many of you had heard the same thing. My mom went on to say that size doesn't matter anyway, but I told her I heard that it matters to girls. Thus the reason I was able to include it. I really just wanted to see if I could write the word penis in my book. I actually looked up alternate names for a penis on the Internet and found a site that listed 101 of them. Mom told me that we weren't writing a thesaurus and for this book I am limited to calling it by its scientific name: penis.

Anyway, getting back to the story, apparently both are myths, the soda pop causing shrinkage and size mattering to girls. Mom quickly told me that, at 13, you shouldn't be worried about any of this for several reasons: Your penis hasn't stopped growing; a girl shouldn't be seeing it; and if she really likes you it shouldn't matter anyway (when you get old enough for that kind of stuff). Does that make any sense? When I write the next book I will add more detail, because you (and I) will be older and more mature (maybe), so you (and I) will be able to handle it without laughing. For now, I'll just stick to some basic information.

At our age, it's hard to control your penis, because it may get excited (the scientific word for this state is an erection) with (or about) almost every girl you see, but you can't start kissing them all. This is a very natural and normal thing. Again, it goes back to biology. If none of this is happening yet, don't worry. Everyone is different in terms of the age they start getting erections and in terms of what excites them. Your penis will show happiness soon enough. Did you ever notice that the word "penis" is actually part of the word happiness? It's just spelled differently. I wonder if it was a boy who invented the word. Distracted again…

Okay, back to girls. It is important not to let your penis do the talking (that is, tell you which girl it likes). By this I mean, don't let the physical feeling you get when you meet a girl make you forget all of the info I gave you in the last eight chapters – most importantly, choosing the girl. Sometimes the attraction is so great that you want to kiss her right away. Afterwards, you might ask, "What was I thinking?" This doesn't mean she's not a nice person, but maybe just not the right one for you. It's a good idea to take the time to get to know a girl before you actually kiss. You also have to pay extra attention to Chapter 4 – "Trust me… Honest." Sometimes you may forget that you already have a special girl you wanna kiss. Kissing someone else could cause really hurt feelings.

Apparently I can't say too much more about penises, since 12-year-olds are my target audience and there are rules about this. Personally I think you should get the facts straight up (no pun intended) from me, rather than finding them on the Internet. Whatever you do, if in doubt ask someone who knows how to tell if something is fact or myth. Trust me, it isn't rocket science – actually I think rocket was one of the 101 names, so maybe it is rocket science – okay Mom, I'll stop… Just adding a little humour. Relax!

***

I know I said I was going to keep this chapter light, but there's another myth, a more serious myth, that Mom says I need to talk about. The myth is that if a girl is wearing certain types of clothing, or if she flirts with you or looks at you a certain way, it means she wants to be kissed and that she deserves less respect than other girls. Again, **NOT TRUE**. As I mentioned earlier, girls are constantly trying to learn about who they are. They are getting used to their changing bodies too. The Internet, media, music, and movies often portray girls in a certain way – the good ones versus the bad ones. But it's not really about good or bad at all. The way a person dresses doesn't make them good or bad. They are often just trying to be themselves. Be an individual. Be real. Mom says that, at times, girls are confused. They want to be liked and fit in and may not know how to do this. They may want attention or they might just like wearing certain clothes. When boys get together, they sometimes show disrespect towards girls who wear tight shirts and short skirts. They may tell each other that "she" really wants to be kissed and encourage each other to try to kiss her. Sometimes they might gang up on her. It is totally wrong and hurtful to trick or force a girl into being kissed. "**NO**" means "**NO!**" – No matter what a girl wears!

Although "**NO**" means "**NO!**" seems like a simple concept, surprisingly there are still those who don't get it. It can be very tricky. Do you ask for permission every time you wanna kiss a girl? Won't that interrupt the moment? Mom says that asking a girl if you can kiss her is a good idea, but even if she says yes, she might change her mind partway through. Apparently your intuition (your hunches) will guide you, but the rule remains:

If you try to kiss her and she says, "No," at any time, then stop. A girl is the only one who knows if she really wants to be kissed. You have to listen to her or there will be bad consequences for both of you. The songs out there may give mixed messages about what a girl wants, but this is often wishful thinking. Sorry guys, there's no humour around this myth.

That was a bit intense – time for a break –
ONE MORE CHAPTER –YEAH!!!!!!!!

CHAPTER 10
Ready, Set, Go **SLOW**

To make it super easy for you, I've summarized all of the chapters into a brief acronym (that's a word formed by combining the first letters of a series of words). It's much easier and convenient to remember **LPSLAAYERS** than it is to memorize ten chapters. It also can be written on your arm to remind you of the important points when you go out with a girl. Don't forget, it's my nickname, with an "S" at the end, so you know whom to thank when it all works out. ☺

Here it is...

L ike yourself – you're a pretty cool dude.

P ick a nice one.

S mell good or not at all.

L ying sucks.

A ccept her moods, she'll like you tomorrow
(but remember not to accept abuse).

A pologize with meaning.

Y ou need your friends; don't let jealousy get in the way.

E xpress yourself – communicate, celebrate, but
don't criticize.

R ead facts not myths, and...

S tart slow.

Now you are ready to go – **SLOW**. Fortunately, we have the advantage these days of getting to know girls pretty well, because of things like texting, Facebook, and Twitter, before we actually date them. Sometimes there are disadvantages to social media, as everyone finds out everything quickly. This can suck if you do something you'd rather no one knows about, but overall, I think it has some advantages over "the olden days." Mom told me that her first boyfriend lived at the other end of the city and she only saw him once every two weeks. She would call him from school on a pay-phone every lunch hour. That was the only place she could have a private conversation, because at home her corded phone was in the kitchen. I can't believe that was only thirty-two years ago. Nowadays there's constant communication, to a point where I say, "How can I miss you when you never leave me alone?" I think that was a title of an old country song, but it seems to make more sense these days.

My last words of advice are that there isn't one formula to finding and keeping a girl you wanna kiss. What I've written is just a guide, based on what I've heard or experienced. Apparently some of the fun of pursuing girls is the fumbling around like an idiot. Yeah, sounds like fun to me. Anyway, it is all learning. I guess we have our whole lives to practise. When you think about it, we spend endless hours practising a sport, in my case soccer, when we have an hour and a half game once a week for eight months of the year, but we spend much less time learning about girls, when we may live with them for the rest of our lives. You will have your own experiences and questions, and I'd love to hear about them. Who knows? Maybe I'll use them in my next book. I'm planning on setting up a blog. I'll keep you posted. In the meantime, enjoy the adventure and don't beat yourself up too much.

LPslaayer out!

Okay Mom, I'm done... now onto something I wanna do. Yeah, I guess parts of it were a little fun... at least the research! (Wink, wink!!)

P.S. I will actually have lots of screen time now, 'cause my mom is making my sister write, *So you Wanna Kiss a Boy....* It's only fair and fairness is everything when it comes to siblings. Haha Katie has a boyfriend!

ACKNOWLEDGEMENTS

To my son, Peter, for being open to learning about girls and providing ideas and humour for the content of this book, and to my daughter, Abbey, who taught me modern lingo and helped me find a younger voice. You are both my inspiration. Thanks for encouraging me to "Just do it!!"

To my husband, Bob, who has shown me what a healthy, loving relationship looks like. Thank you for continually supporting me in the fulfillment of my dream.

To my long-time friend Linda, who has shared many memories with me since *we* were the young teenagers confused about the opposite sex. Thank you for being the first person to critique my book and give me honest feedback – your ongoing input has been invaluable.

To my illustrator Chuck Macintosh for bringing all of the characters to life. You depicted Liam perfectly from the beginning. Thank you for your talent and patience.

To everyone else at FriesenPress who has assisted in the production of this book. I could not have done it without you.

To my friends and family, who have patiently listened to me talk about this book for the past six years. I am very lucky to have such genuine beings in my world.

ABOUT THE AUTHOR

Chris Gaucher was born in Regina, Saskatchewan and currently lives in Victoria, BC. She is a writer who holds degrees in both psychology and dentistry. Chris started writing this book when her son was 11. She wanted to find a way to educate him about the often confusing world of boy/girl relationships in a way that he would be receptive to. Along the way she decided she would try to reach a wider audience.

Printed in Canada